Rip's Secret Spot

Rip's Secret Spot

Kristi T. Butler
Illustrated by Joe Cepeda

Green Light Readers
Harcourt, Inc.
Orlando   Austin   New York   San Diego   London

Pat could not find her frog.

"Who has my frog?"

Mom could not find her pin.
"Who has my pin?"

Dad could not find his hat.
"Who has my hat?"

Pat, Mom, and Dad looked
for the missing things.

"Pat," called Dad, "look at Rip.
He ran off fast."

"Rip is sniffing the grass.
Now he is digging."

"That dog digs all the time," said Pat.

"My hat is in that hole," said Dad.
"There is my frog!" shouted Pat.

"My pin is there, too," said Mom.
"All our things are there!"

"I think that's Rip's secret spot!"
said Dad.

"Let's dig up our things," said Pat.
"We will put *this* in the hole for Rip!"

Guess My Pet!

**You have met Pat's pet dog, Rip.
Write a riddle about a pet you love.**

WHAT YOU'LL NEED

paper

pen or pencil

1. Think of a pet.

2. Write three clues about
the pet.

3. Trade clues with
a friend.

It is green.

It eats bugs.

It is smaller than a book.

4. Read the clues.

5. Try to guess the pet!

A Book Full of Pets

Pat loves her dog, Rip.
What are your favorite pets?

WHAT YOU'LL NEED

- paper
- crayons or markers
- tape
- pencil
- stapler

1. Think about one of your favorite pets.

2. Draw a picture of the animal.

3. On another piece of paper, write the things you like about the animal. Tell why you would like to have that kind of pet.

4. When you are done, tape the two pieces of paper together.

I like fish.
They swim.
They are pretty
to watch.

I love dogs.
They play with you and
they are good friends.
My dog licks my
face all the time.

5. Think of other pets you like.
Draw pictures and write about them, too.

6. When you are done, make a cover
and staple all of the pages together.
Now you have your own book full
of pets!

My
BOOK
Of Pets

Meet the Illustrator

Joe Cepeda reads a story many times before he works on the pictures for it. He doesn't start drawing until he knows the story well. First he draws the place where the story happens. He draws the people last. He likes to make the characters look like people he really knows!

www.HarcourtBooks.com

First Green Light Readers edition 2000
Green Light Readers is a trademark of Harcourt, Inc., registered in the
United States of America and/or other jurisdictions.

The Library of Congress has cataloged an earlier edition as follows:
Butler, Kristi T.
Rip's secret spot/Kristi T. Butler; illustrated by Joe Cepeda.
p.   cm.
"Green Light Readers."
Summary: When Pat, Mom, and Dad mysteriously lose some of their things, the
family dog helps find them.
[1. Dogs—Fiction.   2. Lost and found possessions—Fiction.]   I. Cepeda, Joe, ill.
II. Title.
PZ7. B97735Ri   2000
[E]—dc21   99-50802
ISBN 978-0-15-204809-9
ISBN 978-0-15-204849-5 (pb)

LEO   10 9 8 7
4500342049

Ages 4-6
Grade: I
Guided Reading Level: D-E
Reading Recovery Level: 8-9

Green Light Readers
For the reader who's ready to GO!

"A must-have for any family with a beginning reader."—*Boston Sunday Herald*

"You can't go wrong with adding several copies of these terrific books to your beginning-to-read collection."—*School Library Journal*

"A winner for the beginner."—*Booklist*

Five Tips to Help Your Child Become a Great Reader

1. Get involved. Reading aloud to and with your child is just as important as encouraging your child to read independently.

2. Be curious. Ask questions about what your child is reading.

3. Make reading fun. Allow your child to pick books on subjects that interest her or him.

4. Words are everywhere—not just in books. Practice reading signs, packages, and cereal boxes with your child.

5. Set a good example. Make sure your child sees YOU reading.

Why Green Light Readers Is the Best Series for Your New Reader

● Created exclusively for beginning readers by some of the biggest and brightest names in children's books

● Reinforces the reading skills your child is learning in school

● Encourages children to read—and finish—books by themselves

● Offers extra enrichment through fun, age-appropriate activities unique to each story

● Incorporates characteristics of the Reading Recovery program used by educators

● Developed with Harcourt School Publishers and credentialed educational consultants